THE U.S. ARMY

INSIDE THE U.S. MILITARY

Rosen Publishing

BY TANNER BILLINGS

Library of Congress Cataloging-in-Publication Data

Names: Billings, Tanner, author.
Title: The U.S. Army / Tanner Billings.
Description: New York : Rosen Publishing, 2022. | Series: Inside the U.S. military | Includes index.
Identifiers: LCCN 2019057145 | ISBN 9781978518582 (library binding) | ISBN 9781978518575 (paperback) | ISBN 9781978518599 (ebook)
Subjects: LCSH: United States. Army--Juvenile literature.
Classification: LCC UA25 .B55 2022 | DDC 355.00973--dc23
LC record available at https://lccn.loc.gov/2019057145

Published in 2022 by The Rosen Publishing Group, Inc.
29 East 21st Street, New York, NY 10010

Copyright © 2022 Rosen Publishing

Designer: Sarah Liddell
Editor: Kate Mikoley

Photo credits: Cover, background used throughout Dakin/Shutterstock.com; p. 4 MatthewVanitas/Wikimedia Commons; p. 5 Lennart Priess/Stringer/Getty Images News/Getty Images; p. 7 Shushruth/Wikimedia Commons; p. 9 DEA PICTURE LIBRARY/Contributor/De Agostini/Getty Images; p. 11 Scott Nelson/Stringer/Getty Images News/Getty Images; p. 12 lauradyoung/E+/Getty Images; pp. 13 (all insignia), 24 (Major General, Lieutenant General, General) Illegitimate Barrister/Wikimedia Commons; p. 15 Liesl Marelli of Girona Consulting Inc/Moment/Getty Images Plus/Getty Images; p. 18 Bloomberg/Contributor/Bloomberg/Getty Images; p. 19 Fæ/Wikimedia Commons; p. 21 Hulton Archive/Stringer/Hulton Archive/Getty Images; p. 24 (Second Lieutenant, First Lieutenant) Yaddah/Wikimedia Commons; p. 24 (Captain, Brigadier General, General of the Army) Officer781/Wikimedia Commons; p. 24 (Major, Lieutenant Colonel) Ipankonin/Wikimedia Commons; p. 24 (Colonel) AndreyKva/Wikimedia Commons; p. 25 Bettmann/Contributor/Bettmann/Getty Images; p. 27 Ariel Skelley/DigitalVision/Getty Images; p. 29 Lt. Zachary West/Army National Guard/Getty Images News/Getty Images; p. 31 Jeff Greenberg/Contirbutor/Universal Images Group/Getty Images; p. 34 Alex Wong/Staff/Getty Images News/Getty Images; p. 35 Scott Olson/Staff/Getty Images News/Getty Images; p. 38 Joe Raedle/Staff/Getty Images News/Getty Images; p. 41 Chung Sung-Jun/Stringer/Getty Images News/Getty Images; p. 43 MediaNewsGroup/Orange County Register via Getty Images/Contributor/MediaNews Group/Getty Images; p. 45 tropicalpixsingapore/iStock/Getty Images Plus/Getty Images.

Portions of this work were originally authored by Mark A. Harasymiw and published as *Army*. All new material this edition authored by Tanner Billings.

All rights reserved. No part of this book may be reproduced in any form without permission in writing from the publisher, except by a reviewer.

Printed in the United States of America
Some of the images in this book illustrate individuals who are models. The depictions do not imply actual situations or events.

CPSIA compliance information: Batch #BSRYA22: For further information contact Rosen Publishing, New York, New York at 1-800-237-9932.

CONTENTS

Serving the Country 4

Chapter One: The Army Through History. .6

Chapter Two: Forming Famous Leaders. .16

Chapter Three: Ways to Serve 26

Chapter Four: Into the Army. 36

Glossary 46

For More Information 47

Index. 48

Words in the glossary appear in **bold** type
the first time they are used in the text.

SERVING THE COUNTRY

As long as history has been recorded, groups of people have gone to war with each other. Countries fight over land, **natural resources**, and other matters. Many modern militaries are always ready to fight if they need to protect themselves or their **allies**.

EACH BRANCH OF THE MILITARY HAS A DIFFERENT FUNCTION. SOME BRANCHES PROTECT THE COUNTRY IN THE WATER OR AIR. THE ARMY FOCUSES ON LAND OPERATIONS.

The military forces of the United States exist to protect the country's citizens and interests. The five branches of the armed forces in the United States are the army, navy, air force, coast guard, and marine **corps**. The army is the largest branch. It's also the oldest. It began even before the United States was a country!

CHAPTER ONE: THE ARMY THROUGH HISTORY

In 2020, the U.S. Army celebrated its 245th anniversary, although much about the army has changed in those years. In 1775, the American colonies were fighting a revolution against Great Britain. The colonies had long depended on **militias** for protection against opposing forces. All men were required to serve with their local militia when they were needed.

At the beginning of the American Revolution, colonial leaders realized a more organized and united army was needed to fight the British. On June 14, 1775, the Continental army was created out of several large militias. Less than a month later, George Washington was officially in command of this new army. At the end of the American Revolution, British forces surrendered to the United States, largely due to the success and power of the Continental army.

THIS IMAGE SHOWS A GROUP OF SOLDIERS IN THE CONTINENTAL ARMY DURING THE AMERICAN REVOLUTION.

After the American Revolution, the Founding Fathers disagreed about the future of the victorious Continental army. Some wanted to break it up and go back to the militia system. However, the U.S. Constitution, written in 1787, established that a national army would exist in peacetime as well as during wartime.

IN CIVILIAN HANDS

The Founding Fathers worried that a national army could end up being so strong it would take rights away from citizens. To make sure this didn't happen, they decided that the military needed to be under civilian control. The president, a civilian, holds the army's highest position, commander in chief. Congress, a civilian body, controls the money for the armed forces and has the power to declare war. If a president wants to declare war, they need approval from Congress. The separation of responsibilities makes sure no one person has complete control of the military and ensures it stays under civilian control.

CIVILIAN: A PERSON NOT ON ACTIVE DUTY IN THE MILITARY

 EXPLORE MORE

WASHINGTON BELIEVED THE COUNTRY NEEDED AN ARMY EVEN DURING PEACETIME. HE THOUGHT THAT, RATHER THAN STATES HAVING THEIR OWN MILITIAS, ONE ORGANIZED AND SIMILARLY TRAINED ARMY WOULD BE BEST.

CONGRESS IGNORED WASHINGTON'S ADVICE TO KEEP A CENTRAL MILITARY FORCE. MOST SOLDIERS WERE LET GO IN 1783. BY THE TIME WASHINGTON BECAME PRESIDENT IN 1789, HOWEVER, THE FORCE WAS BACK TO NEARLY 600 MEN.

Today, the U.S. Army is made up of about 687,000 soldiers. Around 487,000 of these people are active duty. Being active duty means the army is your full-time job. Nearly 200,000 soldiers are in the Army Reserve. Reservists generally serve in the army part-time, but they may be called to active duty when the number of active duty soldiers isn't enough to respond to a conflict or situation.

Members of the army may be either **enlisted** soldiers or officers. Among the officers, there are commissioned officers and warrant officers. Each group receives special training and has particular responsibilities. Enlisted soldiers have many different jobs, but all are tasked with completing missions and following orders. Enlisted soldiers can move up the ranks, or positions, to become officers too. Enlisted soldiers of certain higher ranks are called noncommissioned officers (NCOs).

 EXPLORE MORE

ENLISTED SOLDIERS MAKE UP ABOUT 80 PERCENT OF THE ARMY. COMMISSIONED OFFICERS MAKE UP ABOUT 17 PERCENT, AND WARRANT OFFICERS MAKE UP JUST 3 PERCENT.

AN ENLISTED SOLDIER'S JOB IS CALLED A "MILITARY OCCUPATIONAL SPECIALTY," OR MOS. EACH MOS HAS A CODE. FOR EXAMPLE, AN INFANTRYMAN'S MOS CODE IS 11B.

INFANTRYMAN: A PERSON WHO IS A SOLDIER TRAINED TO FIGHT ON FOOT

Commissioned officers are leaders who plan missions and command units. You need a college degree to become a commissioned officer. Warrant officers are experts in their field. They focus on their own specialty and often help train other soldiers to be great at it as well. A soldier who becomes highly skilled in their field may be invited to attend Warrant Officer Candidate School and become a warrant officer.

ENLISTED RANK INSIGNIA

PRIVATE

PRIVATE FIRST CLASS

SPECIALIST

CORPORAL

STAFF SERGEANT

SERGEANT FIRST CLASS

MASTER SERGEANT

SERGEANT MAJOR

COMMAND SERGEANT MAJOR

SERGEANT MAJOR OF THE ARMY

SERGEANT

FIRST SERGEANT

ARMY SOLDIERS WEAR A PATCH WITH THEIR INSIGNIA, WHICH IS A MARKING THAT SHOWS THEIR RANK.

ARMY UNITS

The U.S. Army is organized into units of varying sizes that work together. The smallest unit is the squad. There are around 10 soldiers in a squad. Several squads make up a platoon, while several platoons make up a company, and several companies make up a battalion. Together, several battalions form a brigade, which usually includes at least 2,000 soldiers. Several brigades form a division, and two or more divisions form a corps. A corps is usually the largest tactical unit in the army, but during war, two or more corps may be combined to form a larger unit called a field army.

TACTICAL: HAVING TO DO WITH ACCOMPLISHING A MILITARY GOAL

SQUADS MAY BE DIVIDED INTO TWO FIRE TEAMS, EACH WITH THEIR OWN TEAM LEADER.

CHAPTER TWO: FORMING FAMOUS LEADERS

George Washington wasn't the only army leader who later became a U.S. president. Andrew Jackson was a famous general in the War of 1812. He was elected president in 1828 and was in office until 1837. During the American Civil War, Ulysses S. Grant commanded the Union army to victory against the Confederacy. Grant was elected president in 1868 and was reelected in 1872.

THE AMERICAN CIVIL WAR WAS A WAR BETWEEN THE UNION (NORTHERN STATES) AND CONFEDERACY (SOUTHERN STATES) FROM 1861 TO 1865. EACH SIDE HAD ITS OWN ARMY.

MEDAL OF HONOR

The highest military award given by the U.S. government is the Medal of Honor. In the 1860s, Congress created the award for heroic Union soldiers serving in the American Civil War. Today, the award is given to soldiers who commit a great act of valor while fighting enemy soldiers. The president presents the Medal of Honor to the soldier. To date, Theodore Roosevelt is the only president to receive a Medal of Honor of his own. The award was for his actions in 1898 during the Spanish-American War, but it was given in 2001, more than 80 years after his death.

VALOR: BRAVERY DURING TIMES OF DANGER, ESPECIALLY WAR

THE ARMY AND AIR FORCE EACH HAVE THEIR OWN MEDAL OF HONOR. A THIRD MEDAL IS GIVEN TO MEMBERS OF THE NAVY, MARINE CORPS, AND COAST GUARD.

Another famous U.S. general who would later become president was Dwight D. Eisenhower. Eisenhower attended the U.S. **Military Academy** and later commanded a training center during World War I (1914–1918). In World War II (1939–1945), he directed the Allied powers to victory over German and Italian forces as supreme commander. Eisenhower was elected president in 1952 and reelected in 1956.

IN 1942, EISENHOWER WAS MADE THE COMMANDER OF U.S. TROOPS IN EUROPE. HE WAS LATER MADE SUPREME COMMANDER OF THE ALLIED FORCES.

Most of the war heroes we hear about from early American history are men, but many women have also played key roles in the U.S. military. While today women make up about 15 percent of the army, this hasn't always been the case. Women have been officially serving in the army for **decades**. Before 2015, they weren't allowed to have jobs in combat positions. Still, women have long played important roles in the U.S. Army.

During the American Revolution, women were allowed to serve as nurses but not as soldiers. However, some women dressed as men in order to fight in the war. This continued during the American Civil War, with more than 400 women pretending to be men to fight in the war, and many others working as nurses, aides, and spies.

DISCHARGE: TO OFFICIALLY END SOMEONE'S SERVICE IN THE MILITARY

DURING THE AMERICAN REVOLUTION, A WOMAN NAMED DEBORAH SAMPSON DISGUISED HERSELF AS A MAN TO ENLIST IN THE ARMY. WHEN SHE WAS HURT IN BATTLE, A DOCTOR FOUND OUT SHE WAS A WOMAN AND SHE WAS DISCHARGED.

In 1901, the U.S. Army Nurse Corps was created. During World War I, women served again as nurses, but they also served in many other positions, including as telephone operators and **architects**. However, these women were not officially considered part of the service, or military force, and did not receive the same benefits that men in service did. During World War II, women were officially allowed to serve in groups other than the Nurse Corps. The Women's Army Corps was formed and gave women military status.

★ EXPLORE MORE ★

THE WOMEN'S ARMY AUXILIARY CORPS (WAAC) WAS FORMED IN 1942. THE FOLLOWING YEAR, A UNIT CALLED THE 149TH POST HEADQUARTERS COMPANY BECAME THE FIRST GROUP FROM THE WAAC TO SERVE OVERSEAS.

AUXILIARY: REFERRING TO CIVILIAN VOLUNTEERS WHO PROVIDE SUPPORT TO THE MILITARY WHEN NEEDED

RANKING THE OFFICERS

Depending on their rank, officers in the U.S. Army may be a lieutenant, captain, major, lieutenant colonel, or colonel. Above colonels are generals. The first general rank is brigadier general, then comes major general and lieutenant general. Typically, the fourth type of general is simply called a general. However, the officer may sometimes be called a four-star general. This is because their insignia has four stars. A four-star general usually has more than 30 years of service with the army. In 2008, Ann Dunwoody became the first woman to become a four-star general in the U.S. Army.

OFFICER RANK INSIGNIA

SECOND LIEUTENANT

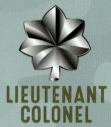
LIEUTENANT COLONEL

LIEUTENANT GENERAL

FIRST LIEUTENANT

COLONEL

GENERAL

CAPTAIN

BRIGADIER GENERAL

GENERAL OF THE ARMY

MAJOR

MAJOR GENERAL

GENERAL OF THE ARMY IS A RANK USED ONLY DURING WARTIME WHEN A COMMANDING OFFICER NEEDS TO BE THE SAME OR HIGHER RANK THAN THOSE FROM OTHER COUNTRIES.

The first female general in the army was Anna Mae Hays. President Nixon awarded her the rank of brigadier general in 1970. Hays had entered the Army Nurse Corps in 1942. She served in India during World War II and in South Korea during the Korean War.

ELIZABETH P. HOISINGTON (LEFT) WAS THE ARMY'S SECOND FEMALE GENERAL. SHE WAS PROMOTED AT THE SAME CEREMONY AS HAYS (RIGHT).

CHAPTER THREE: WAYS TO SERVE

There are different ways to serve in the army. Some soldiers work overseas, while others perform their jobs stateside. For some people in U.S. military service, the army is their full-time job. For others, it's a part-time job.

Active duty soldiers are in the army full-time, while those in the Army Reserve work for the army part-time and often have another career. People who join the Army Reserve must meet the same requirements as other people who join the army. Reservists complete basic training just like soldiers going into active duty positions do. Reservists also receive advanced training to prepare for particular jobs.

IN ADDITION TO THEIR JOB IN THE ARMY, A RESERVE SOLDIER CAN GO TO COLLEGE FULL-TIME OR HAVE A CIVILIAN CAREER.

27

★ EXPLORE MORE ★

ACTIVE DUTY SOLDIERS ARE USUALLY THE ONES TO BE DEPLOYED OVERSEAS. RESERVE SOLDIERS WILL TAKE OVER THEIR JOBS IN THE UNITED STATES TO FILL VACANT POSITIONS. HOWEVER, SOMETIMES THERE IS SUCH A GREAT NEED OVERSEAS THAT RESERVE SOLDIERS ARE DEPLOYED.

DEPLOY: TO MOVE TROOPS INTO A POSITION OF READINESS

After training, reservists can live anywhere in the United States. They're on duty for one weekend a month. Throughout the year, they take part in two weeks of training. At these times, the reservists review what they learned in basic training and advanced training. This helps them stay prepared in case their country needs them, and they're called to active duty.

Another group of soldiers serving part-time in the army is the Army National Guard. During wartime, the National Guard fights right along with the regular army. However, during peacetime, the National Guard conducts rescue operations after emergencies such as severe storms or floods.

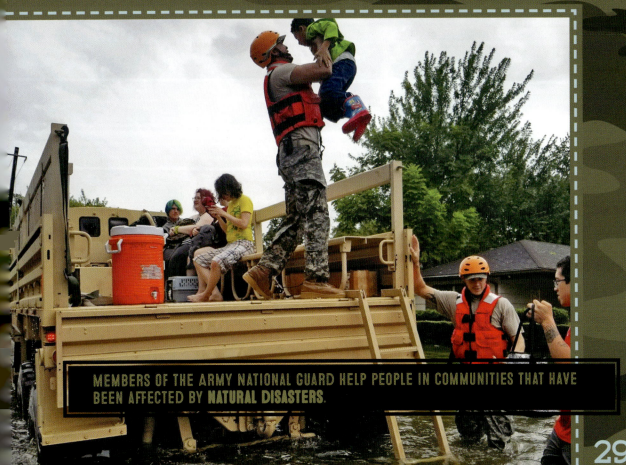

MEMBERS OF THE ARMY NATIONAL GUARD HELP PEOPLE IN COMMUNITIES THAT HAVE BEEN AFFECTED BY **NATURAL DISASTERS**.

JOBS OUTSIDE OF COMBAT

Combat jobs are a key part of the army, but the force wouldn't be able to run without people doing other tasks. The army has jobs in more than 150 different fields. An army base needs everything a city needs. It needs electricians and plumbers for building maintenance, and firefighters and police officers to keep people safe. Doctors, nurses, and dentists keep soldiers healthy in peacetime as well as in war. The army needs mechanics to make sure vehicles are safe. It also needs computer experts, cooks, lawyers, and language specialists. There's a job for nearly every skill and interest.

VEHICLE: AN OBJECT USED FOR CARRYING OR TRANSPORTING PEOPLE OR GOODS, SUCH AS A CAR, TRUCK, OR AIRPLANE

THE ARMY HAS SEVERAL MUSIC BANDS OF VARIOUS SIZES. THESE BANDS NEED SINGERS, TUBA PLAYERS, GUITAR PLAYERS, DRUMMERS, TRUMPET PLAYERS, AND MANY MORE MUSICIANS!

Even among the active duty forces, there are many different ways to serve. The U.S. Army Special Forces—known as the Green **Berets**—are some of the most highly trained people in the U.S. military. They must meet strict requirements and be able to complete very tough training. Green Berets have to be in excellent physical condition and be highly intelligent.

Green Berets may be sent to other countries to gather information or track an enemy's movements. They fight terrorism and train other countries' armies. They may be sent to rescue ally soldiers in danger. Other missions include capturing or destroying a target, such as an enemy base.

TERRORISM: THE CONTINUOUS USE OF VIOLENCE AND FEAR TO SCARE PEOPLE AS A WAY TO ACHIEVE A POLITICAL GOAL

EXPLORE MORE

THE SPECIAL FORCES UNIT FORMED IN 1952. THE NICKNAME, GREEN BERETS, COMES FROM THE HATS THEY BEGAN WEARING IN 1954 TO SEPARATE THEMSELVES FROM THE REST OF THE ARMY.

Another special operations force within the U.S. Army is the 75th Ranger Regiment, commonly know as the Army Rangers. The Rangers' main mission is to fight enemy soldiers in high-risk situations. Though they are all volunteers, they must be selected before receiving intense combat training. Army Rangers face some of the most challenging situations imaginable. The four Ranger battalions are always prepared to fight and defend their country.

WHILE THE SPECIAL FORCES HAVE THEIR GREEN BERETS, ARMY RANGERS WEAR TAN BERETS TO SEPARATE THEMSELVES FROM OTHER SOLDIERS.

A DOG'S GOOD SENSES OF HEARING, SMELL, AND SIGHT ARE HELPFUL DURING ARMY MISSIONS. PLUS, THEY CAN FIT IN SPACES SOLDIERS CAN'T.

ANIMALS OF THE ARMY

Believe it or not, the army needs more than just human workers! The force has jobs for animals too. Dogs are often used in combat situations, sometimes helping units carry out raids. They're also used to patrol army bases. Sled dogs have even been used to help soldiers get around in areas with lots of snow. The army also uses horses for parades and other ceremonies. To take care of all these animals, the army needs people to work as animal trainers and veterinarians. These are great jobs for people who enjoy working with animals and also want to serve their country.

CHAPTER FOUR: INTO THE ARMY

The first step in joining the U.S. Army is meeting with a recruiter. This person's job is to educate people about their choices and help them find answers to important questions. Questions someone looking to join the army needs to ask themselves include: Do I want to be an active duty soldier or a reservist? How long do I want to serve? What job would best suit my skills?

RECRUITER: ONE WHO HELPS A PERSON SIGN UP FOR THE MILITARY

Recruiters are experienced soldiers. Most have had several jobs within the army and have served in different places. People thinking about joining the army should ask their recruiter questions about their own experiences. This will help them learn the truth about what army life is like.

★ EXPLORE MORE ★

THERE ARE MORE THAN 10,000 RECRUITERS FOR THE U.S. ARMY WORKING ALL OVER THE UNITED STATES AND IN OTHER PARTS OF THE WORLD!

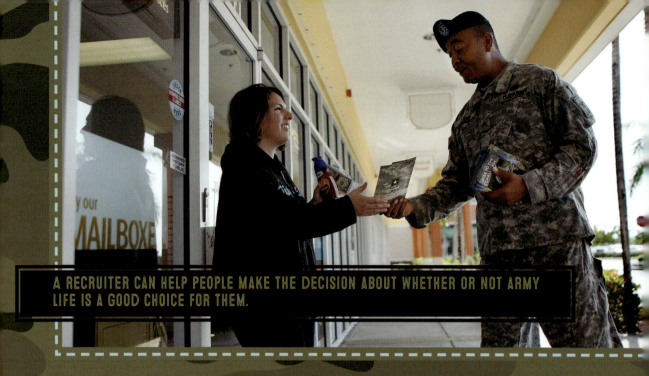

A RECRUITER CAN HELP PEOPLE MAKE THE DECISION ABOUT WHETHER OR NOT ARMY LIFE IS A GOOD CHOICE FOR THEM.

The first introduction into army service is Basic Combat Training (BCT). This is where recruits receive the training needed to become soldiers. It usually lasts about 10 weeks. During BCT, recruits go through serious physical training and are tested mentally. If all goes well, civilians graduate from BCT as soldiers of the U.S. Army.

RECRUIT: A NEWLY ENLISTED SOLDIER

BOOT CAMP PHASES

RED PHASE
RECRUITS RECEIVE HAIRCUTS AND UNIFORMS, AND BEGIN PHYSICAL TRAINING. THEY LEARN TO CONDUCT THEMSELVES AS SOLDIERS AND PROTECT THEMSELVES FROM CERTAIN ATTACKS.

WHITE PHASE
RECRUITS LEARN HOW TO USE A GUN AND PRACTICE SHOOTING AT TARGETS. THEY CONTINUE PHYSICAL TRAINING AND LEARN WHAT A BATTLE IS LIKE.

BLUE PHASE
RECRUITS RECEIVE ADVANCED WEAPONS TRAINING. FOR THE LAST MAJOR TEST OF THEIR SKILLS, THEY MUST NAVIGATE THROUGH A COURSE OVER MULTIPLE DAYS, TESTING THE SKILLS THEY'VE LEARNED.

DURING BCT, OFTEN CALLED BOOT CAMP, RECRUITS GO THROUGH THREE PHASES, OR STAGES, OF TRAINING.

ADVERSITY: A DIFFICULT SITUATION, MISFORTUNE, OR TRAGEDY

ARMY VALUES

In BCT, recruits learn the values of the U.S. Army: loyalty, duty, respect, selfless service, honor, integrity, and personal courage. Recruits learn to live out the meaning of each of these words. Loyalty means being faithful to the country and fellow soldiers. Duty means performing all tasks to the fullest. Respect means treating everyone how they should be treated. Selfless service is putting the needs of your country and others before your own. Honor means living up to all of the army's values. Integrity is always doing what's both legally and morally right. Personal courage is the ability to face fear, adversity, and danger.

THOSE WHO GRADUATE BCT CAN NOW WEAR THE BLACK BERETS OF OFFICIAL ARMY SOLDIERS.

After graduating BCT, soldiers enter Advanced Individual Training (AIT). This is where they learn the skills they need to perform their special job within the army. AIT isn't just about studying—it demands that the soldiers stay in the excellent physical condition they achieved in BCT.

TRAINING IN COLLEGE

The Reserve Officers' Training Corps (ROTC) is a program offered at colleges around the United States. ROTC classes explain the different parts of being a military officer, while also allowing students to take other college courses and earn their degree. ROTC students learn how to be leaders and often receive money to help pay for their college education. A graduate of the Army ROTC program becomes a second lieutenant in the active duty U.S. Army, Army Reserve, or Army National Guard. More than half of the second lieutenants in the army come from the ROTC program.

After entering the force, many soldiers live on an army base. Life here can be very similar to civilian life. When soldiers aren't on duty, they have free time. They spend time on their hobbies, play sports, or catch up with their families.

Many army bases have a store called a commissary. It's much like a grocery store for soldiers and their families. The commissary's size depends on the size of the base. There is also often a store on base called an exchange. These stores are sort of like department stores. Army bases often have movie theaters, barbers, restaurants, and gas stations too.

ABOUT 40 PERCENT OF U.S. ARMY GENERALS CURRENTLY ON ACTIVE DUTY JOINED THE ARMY THROUGH ROTC.

★ EXPLORE MORE ★

MANY ARMY BASES ARE A LOT LIKE REGULAR COMMUNITIES. THEY MAY HAVE REGULAR STREETS WITH SIDEWALKS, PLAYGROUNDS, AND BASKETBALL COURTS.

Many army bases allow soldiers' families to live with them. There are schools for children to attend, libraries, and fitness facilities. Children and parents may join army base sports leagues too. Army families can connect and support each other in times of need, such as when their loved ones serve in foreign countries or are away at war.

HOUSING ON ARMY BASES CAN LOOK SIMILAR TO REGULAR NEIGHBORHOODS IN AREAS THAT ARE NOT PART OF A MILITARY BASE.

GLOSSARY

ally One of two or more people or groups who work together.

architect A person who designs buildings.

beret A round hat with a tight band around the head and a flat, loose top.

corps A group of soldiers trained for special service.

decade A period of 10 years.

enlisted Referring to members of the military who rank below commissioned or warrant officers.

military academy A school for the training of military officers.

militia A group of citizens who organize like soldiers in order to protect themselves.

natural disaster A severe event in nature that commonly results in serious damage and deaths.

natural resource Something in nature that can be used by people.

FOR MORE INFORMATION

BOOKS

Levete, Sarah. *The Army*. New York, NY: Gareth Stevens Publishing, 2016.

Manning, Matthew K. *Two Sides*. North Mankato, MN: Stone Arch Books, 2017.

McDonough, Yona Zeldis. *Courageous: A Novel of Dunkirk*. New York, NY: Scholastic Press, 2018.

Russo, Kristin J. *Surprising Facts About Being an Army Soldier*. North Mankato, MN: Capstone Press, 2018.

WEBSITES

National Museum of the United States Army
thenmusa.org/index.php
Learn more about the U.S. Army on this museum's website.

United States Armed Forces
www.ducksters.com/history/us_government/ united_states_armed_forces.php
Find out more about the different branches of the U.S. military here.

U.S. Army
www.army.mil/
Head to the United States Army's official website to learn more.

Publisher's note to educators and parents: Our editors have carefully reviewed these websites to ensure that they are suitable for students. Many websites change frequently, however, and we cannot guarantee that a site's future contents will continue to meet our high standards of quality and educational value. Be advised that students should be closely supervised whenever they access the internet.

INDEX

A

American Civil War, 16, 17, 20

American Revolution, 6, 8, 20

Army National Guard, 29, 42

Army Nurse Corps, 22, 25

Army Rangers, 33

Army Reserve, 10, 26, 28, 42

B

Basic Combat Training, 38, 40, 41

D

Dunwoody, Ann, 23

E

Eisenhower, Dwight D., 18

G

Grant, Ulysses S., 16

Green Berets, 32, 322

H

Hays, Anna Mae, 25

J

Jackson, Andrew, 16

M

Medal of Honor, 17

militias, 6, 8, 9

R

Reserve Officers' Training Corps (ROTC), 42

W

Washington, George, 6, 9, 16

World War I, 18, 22

World War II, 18, 22, 25